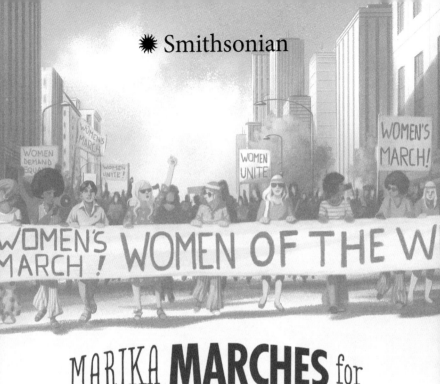

✳ Smithsonian

MARIKA **MARCHES** for EQUALITY

BY SALIMA ALIKHAN
ILLUSTRATED BY ANDREA ROSSETTO

STONE ARCH BOOKS
a capstone imprint

Published by Stone Arch Books, an imprint of Capstone.
1710 Roe Crest Drive
North Mankato, Minnesota 56003
capstonepub.com

The name of the Smithsonian Institution and the sunburst logo are registered trademarks of the Smithsonian Institution. For more information, please visit www.si.edu.

Library of Congress Cataloging-in-Publication Data:
Names: Alikhan, Salima, author. | Rossetto, Andrea, illustrator.
Title: Marika marches for equality / by Salima Alikhan ;
[illustrated by Andrea Rossetto].
Description: North Mankato, Minnesota : Stone Arch Books, an imprint of Capstone, [2022]
| Series: Smithsonian historical fiction | Audience: Ages 8-11. | Audience: Grades 4-6. |
Summary: In 1970 thirteen-year-old Marika dreams of going to Harvard to study economics, but her parents both believe that a woman's place is in the home;
Marika does not understand why they are so attached to "traditional values,"
especially since they defied convention when they were married at a time when interracial marriages were illegal in many states—so Marika defies her parents and joins her Black friend, Beth, and Beth's parents and attends
the Women's Strike for Equality without permission.
Identifiers: LCCN 2021033260 (print) | LCCN 2021033261 (ebook) |
ISBN 9781663911926 (hardcover) | ISBN 9781663921383 (paperback) |
ISBN 9781663911933 (pdf)
Subjects: LCSH: Racially mixed children—Juvenile fiction. | Racially mixed families—Juvenile fiction. | Parent and child—Juvenile fiction. | Women's rights—History—Juvenile fiction. | Demonstrations—History—Juvenile fiction. | CYAC: Women's rights—Fiction. | Demonstrations—Fiction. | Parent and child—Fiction. |
Racially mixed people—Fiction. | LCGFT: Historical fiction. | Novels.
Classification: LCC PZ7.A39696 Mar 2022 (print) |
LCC PZ7.A39696 (ebook)| DDC 813.6 [Fic]—dc23
LC record available at https://lccn.loc.gov/2021033260
LC ebook record available at https://lccn.loc.gov/2021033261

Designer: Sarah Bennett

Our very special thanks to Bethanee Bemis, Museum Specialist, Division of Military and Political History, National Museum of American History, Smithsonian. Capstone would also like to thank Kealy Gordon, Product Development Manager, and the following at Smithsonian Enterprises: Jill Corcoran, Director, Licensed Publishing; Brigid Ferraro, Vice President, Education and Consumer Products; and Carol LeBlanc, President, Smithsonian Enterprises.

TABLE OF CONTENTS

Chapter 1

Tradition

August 24, 1970

With a sigh, Marika put down her pencil. She watched it roll over her finished spelling homework, which was lit by the warm glow of her desk lamp.

Today had been the first day of seventh grade, and she could already tell she was one of the best in her class at spelling. But it wasn't her favorite subject. She always got it out of the way first, so she could save her favorite thing for last—the big book that she had hidden under her mattress.

Marika tiptoed to her door and listened to make sure her parents were still in the living room, watching TV. She could hear her dad all the way down the hall, ranting at something on the news.

"Ridiculous!" he was shouting. "Can't believe it's come to this!"

Marika heard her mom quietly agree in her soft voice. Her mom was from India, and her accent was soothing and gentle.

Marika went to her bed and pulled the heavy book from its hiding spot—her favorite book in the world: *World History of Economics.* Her dad had bought it years ago at a used bookstore.

Marika knew that lots of kids her age would have thought this was the most boring book in the world. But Marika was fascinated by economics. Most people thought "economics" just meant money. But it was *way* more interesting than that. It was about how the whole world worked, and she wanted to know everything she could about that.

She loved learning about what kind of money people used thousands of years ago, and how it had changed over time. Her second favorite thing, besides the book, was her little coin collection. So far she had coins from Spain, Italy, and Japan. She'd never been to any of those places, but having the coins made her feel like she had. Those coins represented the whole wide world that was out there to explore.

Marika sat on her bed and opened the book's heavy cover. She ran her finger down the familiar pages, all the way to the graph that showed economic growth in the United States in the last twenty years. She liked math, but she *loved* graphs and charts.

"Absurd!" her dad bellowed from the living room, making Marika jump. "They'll be disrupting the whole country!"

Marika ignored him. He often got upset about things on the news. She flipped to another page. More than anything, she wanted to go to Harvard University in Massachusetts and study economics. It was one of the best and oldest universities in the country. Marika had wanted to go there ever since she'd seen a TV program about a famous economics professor who had taught there.

But her dad wasn't very excited about that idea. Not Harvard, or any other college.

"It's very difficult for anybody to get into Harvard—but it's especially hard for a girl," he often said. "And besides, there's no reason for young ladies to pursue an education like that, not when they are needed in the home. Who is going to cook and clean and take care of the children if the women all go to work?"

Marika always responded with the same argument. "Lots of women work! I know Mom really likes cooking and housework, but I want other things. I want to go to Harvard and learn all about economics."

But Marika had learned her lesson. She had given up on trying to talk to her parents about her goals, because their opinion never changed. All summer, while her dad was at his job as an accountant and her mom was busy with housework, she'd been sneaking the big economics book off the shelf and reading it in her room. Now that school had started again, she had to sneak it after school and before he came home from work.

She knew they wanted her to do something more "family oriented" than study economics, but she couldn't help it. It was all she wanted to do.

She was just getting settled with the book when she heard her mom say, "It's late. We should tuck Marika in."

Quick as a flash, Marika stuffed the book

back under her mattress, just in time. Her parents cracked open the door.

"Oh good, you're in your pj's already," said her mom.

Marika crawled under the covers and forced a small smile. She wasn't sure she had the energy tonight to debate with her dad if he caught her with the economics book. He wanted her to live safe and sound with them for as long as possible, then grow up and become a housewife, just like her mother had. He certainly didn't want Marika doing anything that might take her far away from home—like an econ degree from Harvard might.

"Would you like a lullaby?" asked her mom.

"I'm too old for lullabies!" Marika said automatically. She didn't know why her parents still insisted on tucking her in, even though she was thirteen now. "What were you watching on TV?" she asked them. "What's 'ridiculous'?"

"Oh, this women's march that will be happening on Wednesday." Her dad made a face. "I don't know what they're thinking, disrupting everything."

Marika sat up in bed. "What women? And why are they marching?"

Her mom shook her head, huffed a small sigh, and said, "They want to give up their traditional values."

Both Marika's parents were into what they called "traditional values"—things like being obedient and respectful to authority, and not causing any trouble. And of course things like women being housewives instead of working outside the home.

"It's as if they don't want to cook and clean for their families anymore," her mom said. "They're going on *strike*! Can you imagine?"

"Maybe they want to take care of their families *and* also have jobs?" Marika suggested quietly.

"They say that women don't have equality," her mom continued, as if she hadn't heard Marika. "As if caring for a family is such a burden. It's the most important job in the world!" She clucked her tongue in disappointment.

"Do they want to go to college?" Marika asked. She took a breath. "That's like me. . . . *I* want to go too."

"Nonsense." Her father smiled like she was being silly. "We've talked about this. You'll come to your senses. There are plenty of things for girls to do besides go to college."

"But I *want* to go!" Marika said, balling her fists under the covers and feeling her energy rise.

"Marika, settle down," her mom said, as if Marika was the one being unreasonable.

Marika found herself wanting to ask her dad, who was white, why he had married an Indian woman, if they were both so concerned with tradition. Marika knew from conversations she had overheard between them that they'd moved from their old neighborhood because some people there didn't tolerate interracial couples. When they'd married in the 1950s, interracial marriages weren't even legal in some states. It wasn't until 1967 that the U.S. Supreme Court decided that laws against interracial marriage were unconstitutional. Even then, some people thought it wasn't right and continued to taunt or attack interracial couples. But her mom and dad had followed their hearts.

So why couldn't Marika follow her own heart and go to college?

"You and Mom didn't do what other people wanted you to do," she said quietly.

"That's enough, Marika," her dad said. "Your mother and I have good reasons for our views on things. We just want what's best for you." He bent to kiss her forehead. "Sleep well."

Marika watched him go, her heart heavy. Then she turned to her mother. "Mom, what's so bad about going to college?"

Her mom furrowed her brows. She pulled the covers up around Marika's shoulders and kissed her forehead too. "We just want life to be easy for you—and safe," she replied. "You'll grow up and have a family, and you'll be happy—you'll see." She gave a small smile, then got up and turned off the light before closing the bedroom door behind her.

Marika tried to calm herself down. She thought of her economics book, buried safely under the mattress. Just knowing it was close helped ease the tension in her shoulders.

She wondered what those marching women really wanted. She had heard about marches before, but she had never seen her parents so upset about one. What was different this time? Was it true that the women wanted to stop caring for their families? If so, why?

Marika decided she was going to find out.

Chapter 2

A Different Set of Values

The next day after school, Marika was just walking down the steps when her friend Beth Williams raced up to her.

"Marika!"

Marika and Beth had been friends since they met last year, when they sat next to each other in Mrs. Gilman's class. Now, Beth was out of breath and her eyes were shining.

"What is it?" asked Marika.

"Want to come over today?" Beth lowered her voice. "We're getting ready for the march!

I know that some people in this town aren't excited about it, but my family is! If you want, you can help!"

Marika froze. "The . . . women's march? That was on the news last night?"

"Yup." Beth nodded proudly. "It's 'The Women's Strike for Equality.' My mom is organizing lots of people in our town who support it. It's been fun. We're doing last-minute stuff tonight, since the march is tomorrow."

Marika blinked in disbelief. All she could think of was the way her parents had talked about the march, like it was something shameful and wrong. "Your parents aren't mad about it?"

Beth laughed. "Mad? Of course not. They're excited about it! You should come over. You can stay for dinner too, if you want."

A little unfamiliar thrill started in Marika's gut. For the most part, she always did what her parents wanted her to do. She'd never lied to them . . . except about the economics book.

But this felt different, somehow. She shuddered. She could only imagine what her parents would say if they knew what Beth's family was doing. And that Marika might join them.

"Okay," Marika said slowly. "I'll come over. I'll just have to call my mom once I get there, to tell her where I am."

"Great! Let's go!" said Beth.

They walked to Beth's house, which was just a few blocks away from Marika's. Marika had been to Beth's house a few times. But even before they walked into the house, Marika could tell it was going to be different this time. Today there was lots of noise inside the Williams' house—music from a record player, laughter, and happy voices. As Marika and Beth climbed the front steps, a woman came out of the front door, the screen door banging behind her.

"Mrs. Naylor!" said Beth cheerfully. "How's it going in there?"

"Your mom's got us all working our fingers to the bone!" the woman said cheerfully. "But there's no better cause. Who's your friend here?"

"This is my friend Marika O'Dell," said Beth. "She wants to help."

"Great! We need more young women to get involved!" said Mrs. Naylor. "I'll be right back—just picking up dinner for the crew. Looks like it'll be pizza tonight!"

"Sounds delicious! Thanks!" Beth said. Then she pulled Marika into the house. "Come meet everybody."

Just like Marika had guessed, she walked into a scene that would never, ever have happened at her own house. There were about ten women inside. Some walked around carrying boxes and papers. Others sat drawing, writing, or talking around the living room, which was a colorful mess of posters, paint, and signs. People dashed around asking for scissors and other supplies. Marika could hear someone in another room saying, "We would *love* the local news station to cover our town's march on Wednesday. Please let us know if you can make it!"

Marika noticed that a few of the women were Black, like Beth. But there was an Asian woman there too, and one who looked Latina. And some who looked biracial, like Marika. It made her happy to see all kinds of women in this room. In their town, Marika mostly saw people who were white, like her dad.

A woman carrying a box rushed past Marika. She set it down on the floor. Marika could see what was inside—stacks of flyers that read, *Come Join the Women's March!*

Marika felt shy and a little dazed. She'd never seen so much activity and so many busy women in one place—women who were clearly on a mission.

"Mom, Marika's come over to help!" Beth called. "Can she stay for dinner?"

"Sure!" Beth's mom came out of the kitchen, the phone in her hand stretching on its long cord. Marika realized she was the one she'd heard talking to the news station.

Mrs. Williams smiled warmly at Marika. "Nice to see you, Marika. Excuse the mess around here, but we're glad you've come to help! We're taking care of a few last preparations for the march tomorrow."

Marika shifted on her feet. She felt silly asking, but she still hadn't gotten a real answer from anyone. "Um, why exactly are women marching?"

Beth's mom smiled. "It's for equality. It's to

push for change so that we'll get paid as much as men do, for one thing."

"And to get laws enacted that keep people from discriminating against us," another woman piped up. "So we can do things like get credit cards without our husbands' permission."

"And so that we can get into the colleges we want to go to!" called someone else from the dining room.

Marika felt the breath hitch in her chest. "I want to go to Harvard," she heard herself saying to the group of women.

"Good for you!" one woman declared, pumping her fist in the air. "Right now, they make it *hard* for women to get into Harvard. Only one woman for every four men gets in. But we're going to change that!"

"Marika will get in," Beth said confidently. "She's a whiz at math. She wants to study economics."

Beth's mom smiled even wider. "Well, that's just wonderful! If we have our way, by the time you graduate, girls will have equal access to the colleges they want to go to. I'm proud of you!"

Marika's breath caught again. But this time it was because a grown-up had actually said they were proud of her for *wanting* to go to college. She wished her own parents felt that way.

"You're not alone, kiddo," Beth's mom went on. "Betty Friedan has called for women to march on Wednesday, all over the country. Do you know who she is?"

"No," Marika said, shaking her head.

"Betty Friedan is the founder of the National Organization for Women," said the woman who had brought the box of flyers. "There are thousands, maybe millions, of women who want things to be more fair. We're marching tomorrow in cities all across the country to get people to hear our voices!"

Marika could hardly believe it. *Millions* of women who believed she should be able to be what she wanted?

"But we still have lots of work to do," Beth's mom said. "Why don't you girls help with the signs?"

"Sure, Mom," said Beth. "Come on, Marika."

"I have to call my mom first," Marika said. She used the green phone that hung on the Williams' wall to call her house and let her mom know she was having dinner at Beth's house. As soon as she hung up, the front door opened again and Beth's dad walked in.

Marika's shoulders tightened. She was ready for Beth's dad to get mad about the chaos in the house, the way her dad might. He liked things quiet and orderly, and right now the laughing, talking, busy buzz at Beth's house was anything but quiet.

But Mr. Williams just smiled at the pandemonium.

"Organized chaos, I see!" he said, hugging Beth and her mom. "It's getting crazier and crazier in here. How can I help?"

Marika couldn't believe it. Had she heard him correctly?

"You can help with some of the signs in here, and listen for the phone in case the news station calls back," Beth's mom told him. "I need to help Mary load the flyers into the car so she can take them to the meeting at the community center tonight."

"You got it," Mr. Williams said as he walked into the kitchen and helped himself to a can of soda.

"I don't believe it!" Marika whispered to Beth. "My dad would have been so mad!"

"Really? Why?" Beth asked.

"Well . . . ," Marika said, trying to decide how to explain it. "He's kind of old-fashioned," she finally said.

They grabbed some markers, paints, and two of the big blank poster boards, then sat on an empty part of the living room floor to work.

"Tell him it's 1970!" Beth said with a laugh. "It's time for change. My dad says that since he knows what it's like to be discriminated against because of the color of his skin, he doesn't want to do the same thing to women. He says he wants to fight to make sure I can do anything I want in my life."

Some voices drifted in from the dining room.

"I love my kids, but I love my job too," one of the women was saying. "I shouldn't have to choose."

"I hear you," said another. "Can you believe my boss fired me when he found out I was pregnant? Talk about unfair!"

Marika blinked. She turned to Beth.

"That doesn't sound fair," Marika whispered. "I didn't know women could lose their jobs just because they have kids."

"Definitely not fair," said Beth's mom, who had overheard them. "And we won't have equal opportunity in work, pay, and education until we have affordable childcare for all."

"Women should be able to have kids if they *want* to, without getting punished for it!" Beth said.

Marika sorted through the markers, her head spinning with all these new ideas. She thought about conversations and news stories she'd heard about the Civil Rights marches, which hadn't been that long ago. In those, Black people in the South had fought to end segregation. She had always thought it was horribly unfair that they didn't have the same rights as white people. Especially since her own mom was Indian. Marika knew what it was like to feel different. Her mom and dad had experienced that racial discrimination too. Didn't they understand that holding women back was just another type of discrimination?

Sadness settled over Marika. She wished her own dad was more like Beth's. She wished her dad understood what it felt like to be told you couldn't do something just because you were a girl.

She stared at her blank poster and asked Beth, "What are you going to write on your sign?"

"I'm going to write *WOMEN DESERVE THE SAME RIGHTS!*" said Beth. "What about you?"

Marika thought a moment. "I think I'm going to write *EDUCATION FOR ALL WOMEN!*"

"Groovy!" Beth grinned. "We can hold them high at the march tomorrow!"

"Wait! *We're* going to the march?" Marika dropped the marker she was holding.

Beth laughed. "Of course! What did you think we were doing all this for? Dad's taking me right after school tomorrow. Mom will already be there. She says it's important for my education."

All of Marika's happiness vanished, and she felt miserable again. "My parents definitely won't let me go."

Beth thought a minute. "Maybe they don't need to know. You could just tell them you're coming to my house after school again."

Marika chewed her lip. She wasn't used to lying to her parents. But this felt too important to miss. "Okay," she said slowly. "I really do want to go . . ."

Beth gave a big smile and picked up her

poster. "You won't regret it. Let's make these really colorful so no one can miss them!"

Marika got back to work on her poster. The song on the record player made her want to dance. The living room stayed busy, with people coming and going. Marika couldn't remember a time she'd felt this important. When Mrs. Naylor arrived with the pizzas, everyone paused to eat and joke around, and then it was back to work.

By the time it was beginning to get dark outside, Marika was covered in marker and paint, but she was grinning from ear to ear.

"I should get going and wash this stuff off me before my dad gets home," Marika said.

"Good thinking," said Beth, giving her a hug. "We'll keep your posters over here, and my dad will bring them when he picks us up after school. I can't wait!"

Marika left the busy, happy house, her

feet light. She was dizzy with the idea of *thousands*—maybe *millions*—of women who believed that she should be able to go to college! They believed that girls should be able to do whatever boys could do—and Marika believed that too.

She took a deep breath of the warm evening air. She was going to go to Harvard and become an economist.

Chapter 3

Trouble

With every step Marika took toward her own house, her feet grew a little heavier. When she got to the front yard and saw her dad's car in the driveway, she stopped.

Drat. She'd hoped to make it home before he did.

She gently opened the door and stood in the front hall, listening. Her parents were watching the news in the living room, as usual.

"Is that you, Marika?" her mom called.

"Yes!" Marika scooted toward the bathroom before her parents could see her. "I'm just going to shower real quick. I'm all sweaty!"

As Marika was stuffing her paint-covered clothes under her bed after showering, her mom called, "Want some kulfi?"

Marika loved kulfi, which was kind of like ice cream, but she answered back, "No thanks, I'm stuffed." She didn't want to face her parents right now.

She pushed her door halfway closed and sighed with relief. Her parents would be busy watching the evening news for a little while longer. She'd been so happy to make signs at Beth's house that she couldn't stop herself from making a couple more small ones. She pulled a pad of construction paper off the shelf in her room and settled down on her bed to work. She took out her markers. This time, instead of writing *EDUCATION FOR ALL WOMEN!*, she wrote *COLLEGE IS FOR GIRLS*. After she'd written it on a red piece of paper, she tore out a sheet of blue, and wrote it there too. Maybe she could pass these out at the march tomorrow to people who hadn't made signs.

She smiled to herself as she worked. The idea of the march brought the same excited thrill to her belly that she'd felt that afternoon at Beth's house. She felt like she was part of something big.

She was just finishing up with the blue sheet, when there was a quick knock on her bedroom door. Her dad poked his head into her room. "Marika, no dessert for you?" He glanced at the bright papers on her bed. "What's all this?"

Marika sat up straight. "N-nothing, Dad. It's nothing."

He walked toward the bed, smiling. "Still doing homework?" His smile faded and his brow wrinkled as he read the signs upside down. Then he sighed.

"Marika," he said. "Who put you up to this?"

"No one!" Marika stacked the papers and pulled them toward her. "I decided to do it myself."

Marika's mother came into the room behind her dad. "What's going on, beti?"

"Marika's gotten some ideas into her head," said her dad, furrowing his brow. He picked up one of the papers to show her mom. "Marika, why are you doing this?"

"Dad, it's just—I think I should be allowed to go to Harvard! Or at least apply," Marika said, her own face red now. "It's not fair. Lots of other people—"

"Marika, we talked about this just last night," her mom said. "I know it's easy to get caught up in the crazy things other people are saying."

"It's not crazy! And we didn't *talk* about it.

We never do—you just say no, and then the conversation is over!" said Marika. "What's so bad about wanting to go to college? About girls wanting more than just *tradition*?"

"That's enough." Her dad reached down and took the pieces of paper. "It's time for you to go to bed. You, young lady, are officially grounded."

"Grounded?" Marika cried. She was usually pretty well-behaved and quiet, but she was madder right now than she'd ever been. She raised her voice at her father. "For what? Writing on a piece of paper?"

"For being disrespectful to your parents," her dad said sternly.

"But that means I can't go to the march tomorrow!" Marika blurted.

Her mom's eyes widened. "Of course you won't go to the march! What are you thinking? It could be dangerous! You'll be coming right home after school. And you're not to see that Beth girl."

Her father left the room, the construction paper still in his hand. Her mom followed him, closing the door behind her.

Marika sat on her bed, angry tears streaming down her cheeks. She realized she was shaking. She wanted more than anything to throw her lamp against the door after them, but she knew if she did that she'd be in even bigger trouble.

She thought of how excited she'd felt earlier that day—like she was part of something big and important. For a few hours, she'd been more hopeful than ever before, like her dream might actually be a reality one day.

And now it was over before it had even started.

Chapter 4

A Feeling of Change

The next day at school, Marika felt sick to her stomach. She was afraid if she talked to anyone, she'd start crying.

After school, Beth bounced up to her. "Ready?" she asked, her eyes shining. "Time to go! I'm so excited!"

Marika hung her head, her face flaming. She told Beth about the argument with her parents.

"I don't know what I was thinking," Marika said. "I should have known better." She felt empty and deflated, like the balloon of hope inside her had lost all its air.

Beth looked crushed too. "I'm sorry, that's really hard."

Just then Beth's dad pulled up in his station wagon. "Hi, girls!" he called with a big grin. "Ready to march?"

Suddenly, Marika felt the anger come back. She could see all the signs they'd made piled in the back of the car. Beth's parents were going to march so that girls and women could have equal rights. They believed that girls should have the same opportunities as boys. They wanted Beth to succeed. Didn't Marika's parents want that for their daughter too?

Marika took a deep breath.

"I'm ready," Marika called back. She wasn't sure what had overtaken her, but she found the words coming out of her mouth.

"What do you mean?" asked Beth.

"I'm coming anyway," Marika said, squaring her shoulders.

Beth's eyes widened. "Even though you're grounded?" she whispered.

Marika nodded. "This is worth it." Her belly churned, but she felt sure. "But don't tell your parents I'm not allowed to come."

Beth nodded, a slow smile spreading across her face. "Deal."

"Come on, then, girls," called Beth's dad. "I didn't take the afternoon off work to sit in this car! There's a march waiting for us!"

Marika smiled as she hopped into the back seat with Beth. The whole way to the city center, they talked excitedly about what they might see and how many people might be there.

When Mr. Williams parked the car, Marika heard something. It got instantly louder the moment she opened the door:

chanting, shouting, voices booming through megaphones.

She could feel the energy in the air. She wondered if it was the feeling of *change*.

"Hey, you three!" Beth's mom dashed up to them, her face bright and happy. "Right on time! It's been amazing—let me show you!"

They grabbed their signs and followed Mrs. Williams down the block and to the left, where Marika was overwhelmed at the sight: an entire army of women pouring down the street, holding signs, waving banners, shouting, chanting, laughing, linking arms, and marching together. There were signs everywhere:

WOMEN UNITE!

EQUAL RIGHTS FOR WOMEN, FINALLY!

DON'T COOK DINNER TONIGHT!

One especially caught Marika's eye:

ALL WOMEN DESERVE EDUCATION—
IGNORANCE HURTS EVERYONE!

Marika inhaled sharply. She glanced at Beth, and slowly raised her sign as high as she could.

Beth did the same with her sign.

"You look like you're ready, girls," said Beth's mom, and she raised her own sign. It read, *OUR DAUGHTERS DESERVE BETTER.*

The four of them started marching with the crowd. Marika linked one arm with Beth and waved her sign with the other. She had never in her life imagined she could feel like this—like she was doing something that might change the world, something that was so important for so many people—so important for herself. The people all around her, women and some men, believed she should be able to make her own decisions. They thought she should have the chance to go to any college that boys did, and some day earn just as much money at her job as men. They believed she could be whatever she wanted.

"Free women now!" A chant started up somewhere in the middle of the crowd. The chant caught like wildfire, until soon everyone was shouting, "Free women now!" She glanced at Beth's parents, who held their own signs high, their chins jutting out proudly as they chanted along.

"Look, Marika!" Beth cried, pointing.

Over on the sidewalk, a small crowd had gathered around a podium. A woman stood behind it with a megaphone. The words across the front of the podium were: *EDUCATION FOR AMERICA'S GIRLS!* Clustered around the podium were people holding up signs like *COLLEGE IS FOR EVERYONE, NOT JUST BOYS!* and *EDUCATED WOMEN ARE STRONG WOMEN!*

Marika's eyes widened. Her knees actually felt wobbly.

Beth's mom leaned toward Marika. "See, hon? You're not alone. Lots of people feel this way. Let's go see what that's about."

Nodding, Marika followed Mrs. Williams toward the podium. The woman behind it was shouting, "Equality for all means equal opportunities in education for girls!"

"Education for girls! Education for girls!" chanted the people around her. Marika, Beth, and Beth's parents held up their signs and cheered.

A few people with microphones and cameras joined the small crowd. "We're from Channel 4 News. Would you like to do a quick interview?"

"In a minute," the woman at the podium said. Marika thought she might be imagining it, but it looked like the woman was staring right at Marika. Then she stepped down from the podium and walked right toward her!

"Great sign!" the woman said. "What's your name?"

Marika glanced at Beth's mom for some encouragement. Mrs. Williams smiled and nodded.

"Marika," she answered in a small voice.

"Nice to meet you. I'm Gloria. And what are you protesting for today, Marika?" the woman asked.

"I—I want to go to Harvard," Marika said. Her voice grew stronger.

Gloria's face lit up. "Oh yeah? What do you want to study there?"

Marika swallowed. "Economics."

She waited for Gloria to tell her she was too much of a dreamer, and that the odds were terrible. Instead, Gloria kept smiling.

"Amazing!" Gloria clapped. "Would you like to come on up here and say a few things to the crowd? Tell them why it's important to march for women's rights?"

Marika glanced again at Beth's parents. They were still smiling but looked surprised.

"You don't have to if you're uncomfortable, honey," Beth's mom said to Marika.

Marika blinked around at the crowd, at the women marching for *her* freedoms. Marching so she would have a good future.

She turned back to Gloria. "Okay," she said, swallowing hard.

"You can do it!" Beth squealed, squeezing her hand.

Marika stepped up to the podium, her legs *definitely* wobbling now.

"Here." Gloria handed her the megaphone. "Tell them exactly what you told me. Talk about why you're here, why it's important to you."

Marika cleared her throat. The eyes of the small crowd were on her, and most of the group were smiling. Beth's mom nodded and gave her a thumbs-up.

Marika took a deep breath.

"Um, I'm here . . ." Her voice sounded so loud coming out of the megaphone that it startled her. She took another breath. "I'm here because I want to go to Harvard."

The crowd cheered, which startled her again.

"Tell them what you want to study!" Gloria shouted.

"Economics," said Marika. The crowd cheered again, and her legs steadied a little bit. "I love knowing how things work." No one was yelling at her to be quiet, so she went on. "I think it should be easier for girls to get into good colleges. I think girls shouldn't be told they can't get an education, or don't

need an education. Girls should be allowed to be whatever they want. And I think colleges should—" Marika felt a new, strange heat rise up in her shoulders. "I think colleges should feel *lucky* to have girls who want to learn!"

She didn't even realize she'd had that much to say. The crowd had gone so wild it surprised her. People were shouting, clapping, and snapping photographs of her. Jumping up and down. Cheering, chanting, "Education for women! Education for girls!"

And, she realized with a sickening swoop of her stomach, *the news crew was filming!* Cameras were pointed right at her as she stood there on the podium. Before she had a chance to worry that her parents would see her on the evening news, she saw something even worse.

Her parents were there in person.

Chapter 5

Hope

Marika's whole body froze. She managed to set down the megaphone. As soon as she stepped off the podium, the news crew swarmed her.

"What were you hoping to accomplish today?" one of the reporters asked her, holding his mic to her face.

She could see her parents elbowing their way through the crowd to get to her.

"I—" she stammered. "I wanted to tell people that girls should be able to get into college as easily as boys."

"And why is that so important?" the man pressed.

Marika thought this was a silly question. "Because there's no reason *not* to let girls into colleges. We're just as smart and capable as boys."

"Excuse me." Marika's dad pushed past the news crew, panting. His face was bright red. "Excuse me, *this* is my daughter—"

"Oh, the proud dad!" said Gloria. She came over to shake his hand. "You've got a brilliant young woman here who inspired this crowd!"

His face got even redder. He looked from the woman to Marika. "What do you mean?"

"Well, she told the crowd about wanting to go to Harvard," Gloria said. "She's got a bright future!"

Marika's mom stood next to her dad, looking back and forth between Marika and Gloria with wide eyes.

The reporter turned to Marika's dad. "How does it feel to have your daughter join the protest and speak out?" the man asked. "Are you here in support of the women's strike?"

Marika thought her dad might explode. But he looked nervous too. His gaze darted to the cameras. "I don't see how that's anyone else's business," he muttered. "We're headed home now."

Marika's heart sank. Gloria resumed speaking at the podium, and the news crew turned their attention back to her. Marika and her parents stepped away from the crowd.

Beth's parents made their way over to them. "Good job, Marika!" Mrs. Williams said as Beth hugged Marika.

Marika's dad straightened up. "You took our daughter here without our permission!" he said.

"They didn't know, Dad," Marika explained. "I didn't tell them you grounded me."

"Marika, you can't lie to other people's families!" her mom said.

"I'm sorry I lied," Marika said. But she felt the same anger rising up. Her legs still felt wobbly, but she straightened her shoulders and exclaimed, "But I'm not sorry I came."

"Marika!" said her mom.

"I'm *not*." Marika tried to ignore her trembling legs and planted her feet firmly. "I came because I *do* think girls deserve equal rights and should be able to get whatever education they want. I think it's wrong to tell girls they can't."

She felt the tears stinging her eyes. "I wish you would understand. You both know what it's like to be told you can't do something. You *knew* it was wrong when others said that people of different races shouldn't get married. But you did it anyway, because you love each other. That's how *I* feel. I know it's wrong when people tell me I shouldn't go to college because I'm a girl. I'll do it anyway, because I love learning."

She met her dad's eyes. He was watching her with a look she'd never seen before. Was it shock? Or maybe . . . understanding? Her mom was wiping away tears.

"We'll let you talk with your parents, Marika," said Mrs. Williams. "See you soon, sweetie. Come on, Beth."

Beth gave Marika a sympathetic smile and nod of encouragement, then left with her parents.

Marika faced her mom and dad. Without Beth's family, she felt a lot more alone. And she knew she was in huge trouble.

"You can ground me until I'm eighteen," she said. "I'm still going to Harvard after that."

Marika's dad did something he'd never done before. He bent so he was eye-to-eye with

her. To her shock, his eyes were damp like hers were.

"Marika," he said, "it's very difficult to get into Harvard, even for boys. I don't want you to get hurt or disappointed."

"I don't care if I get hurt," Marika said. "I have to *try*. I'll work hard. I already work hard."

He reached behind him for Marika's mom's hand. "The fact that your mother and I know hardship is the very reason I want to protect you from it. We know how hard it is to go a different way than others, and we don't want you to experience that. It was very difficult when we were first married. Our community didn't accept us, and we had to move to a new neighborhood. I wanted . . ." He blinked very fast. "I want you to have an easier life than we did."

"But I won't have an easy life if I don't get to do what I love. I would always be disappointed," said Marika. "I can do this. I know I can. And if I fail, I'll be proud that at least I tried."

Her mom put a hand on Marika's shoulder.

Her dad looked at her a long time. Finally he said, "I know you can do it."

"What?" Marika thought she hadn't heard right. "What did you say?"

"I said, 'I know you can.'" He wiped his eyes and nodded slowly. "I suppose I'll have to . . ." He looked around at the women still marching, still shouting for freedom. "I suppose I'll have to find a way to support you as much as these women do. And understand that times are changing."

Marika stared at her father in disbelief. Then she said, because she couldn't help herself, "I've been studying the economics book. I sneak it out at night to read. I've already learned so much. I can tell you about everything I've learned!"

Her dad stood up and looked out at the crowd again. Now, he had a different look on his face—like he was seeing a whole new world.

"This is really something," he finally said.

"Can we stay a little longer, Dad?" Marika asked, following his gaze. "Please?"

He looked uncomfortable, but he glanced at her mom and said, "Okay. A little while. As long as things don't get *too* wild."

"And when we go home, can we talk economics? It's really fascinating!" said Marika.

"Dinner first," said Marika's mom.

"Okay, but after that?" asked Marika.

Her dad gave a little smile. "Actually, that sounds like pretty good dinner conversation," he said.

WOMEN'S STRIKE FOR EQUALITY

For generations, women have worked very hard to have equal rights in the United States. As recently as the 1960s and 1970s, women weren't allowed to do many things that they do now. For example, many banks refused to let women have their own credit cards without their husbands' permission. Many colleges didn't start admitting women until the 1970s. Employers were allowed to fire women if they got pregnant, and they were allowed to pay women less than men for the same work. Everywhere, women experienced discrimination.

Some brave and determined women decided to fight back. In 1963, feminist Betty Friedan wrote a book called *The Feminine Mystique,* in which she argued that women should be allowed to be more than wives and mothers if they wanted to be. She, like other feminists, believed that women were just as important and could contribute just as much as men. She believed that in societies where women do not have equal rights, everyone in the society suffers. *The Feminine Mystique* became a huge best seller, proving that many people agreed. Women were tired of being told what they were allowed to do. They wanted the freedom to make their own decisions. Friedan also founded the National Organization for Women, which sponsored the Women's Strike for Equality. On August 26, 1970—the fifty-year anniversary of the 19th Amendment, which granted women the right to vote—Friedan called for women all over the country to strike in protest of the unfair conditions. She asked women to stop cooking and cleaning for the day, and to march together to show the country that they had had enough. She hoped the media would report on the strike so that the issue would get greater attention.

Many people, including the news stations and the police, which were run mostly by men, thought the march was a joke. They did not take it seriously, and they mocked the efforts of women who were protesting. But they were in for a surprise: The march turned out bigger and better than Friedan could ever have hoped. The police in New York City were expecting a small march. They refused to block off the street so that the protesters could march in safety. But when they saw the tide of 50,000 women marching down 5th Avenue, they quickly blocked off the street. At the same time, marches and demonstrations blazed in dozens of cities all over the country. In Boston, 5,000 women gathered. In Washington, D.C., 1,000 women marched. In San Francisco, 2,000 women marched. Other cities like Detroit, Syracuse, St. Louis, and Minneapolis also held protests.

On August 26, 1970, thousands of women marched into history, fighting for the rights and safety of all women. The Women's Strike for Equality was an important moment in American history. It was one of the things that helped put laws into place that protect women. The 1972 Title IX Law and the 1974 Women's Educational Equity Act made it illegal for schools and colleges to discriminate based on gender. The Equal Credit Opportunity Act of 1974 forbade creditors from discriminating against women, and the Pregnancy Discrimination Act of 1978 forbade employers from discriminating against pregnant women. Thanks to feminists like Friedan, girls and women began to be more free.

GLOSSARY

accountant (uh-KOWN-tuhnt)—someone who keeps track of money at a business

beti (BAY-tee)—a common Hindi and Urdu word for daughter

discriminate (dis-KRIH-muh-nayt)—to treat people unfairly because of their race, sex, age, or disability

economics (eh-kuh-NAH-miks)—the study of the way money, goods, and services are made and used in society

equality (eh-KWAH-luh-tee)—the same rights for everyone

feminist (FEM-uh-nist)—someone who believes strongly that women ought to have the same opportunities and rights that men have

ignorance (IG-nor-anss)—the state of lacking knowledge, education, or awareness

interracial (in-tur-RAY-shul)—involving people of different races

kulfi (KUHL-fee)—a South Asian frozen dairy dessert similar to ice cream

pandemonium (PAN-deh-MOH-nee-um)—a wild uproar

unconstitutional (UHN-KON-stuh-TOO-shun-ul)—not in agreement with the Constitution

BECOMING AN ACTIVIST

There are some fun, safe ways you can be an activist just like Betty Friedan. Here are some easy steps.

1. Where do you see a problem? Is there a situation where people are being treated unfairly?

2. If you can, talk to the people being affected. Ask them what they wish was different. This will help you better understand their problem.

3. Brainstorm a solution. How can you help solve it? Do you know anyone who might want to help you?

4. Make a plan. There are lots of different ways to help people. You can make signs supporting the cause you care about. You can donate toys, food, and household items to people who need them. You can write letters to people in power and ask them to change laws. You can raise money with simple things like lemonade stands and bake sales, and then donate to causes you believe in. You can volunteer to help people. And you can march, like Marika did. It feels good to stand up for our own and others' rights.

ABOUT THE AUTHOR

photo by Sam Bond Photography

Salima Alikhan has been a professional writer and illustrator for more than fifteen years. She lives in Austin, Texas, where she is also a college English and Creative Writing professor. She feels very lucky that she still gets to create worlds that other people want to explore.

ABOUT THE ILLUSTRATOR

photo by Federica Gasparella

Andrea Rossetto was born in 1977 in Italy. Drawing has always been his greatest passion. He has worked as an illustrator since 2004 with companies including Disney, Cambridge University Press, Les Humanoïdes Associés, Soleil Editions, and Bamboo. He teaches drawing and digital coloring at the International School of Comics in Padua. He has a wife and a son whom he loves a lot, and a box full of dreams!